D0450968

PUPPY PATROL ™

POSH PUP

BOOKS IN THE 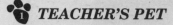 PUPPY PATROL SERIES ™

PUPPY PATROL ™

POSH PUP

JENNY DALE

Illustrations by Mick Reid
Cover illustration by Michael Rowe

AN
APPLE
PAPERBACK

SCHOLASTIC INC.
New York Toronto London Auckland Sydney
Mexico City New Delhi Hong Kong Buenos Aires

If you purchased this book without a cover, you should be aware that this book is stolen property. It was reported as "unsold and destroyed" to the publisher, and neither the author nor the publisher has received any payment for this "stripped book."

No part of this publication may be reproduced in whole or in part, or stored in a retrieval system, or transmitted in any form or by any means, electronic, mechanical, photocopying, recording, or otherwise, without written permission of the publisher. For information regarding permission, write to Macmillan Publishers Ltd., 25 Eccleston Place, London SW1W 9NF and Basingstoke.

ISBN 0-439-31912-9

Text copyright © 1999 by Working Partners Limited.
Illustrations copyright © 1999 by Mick Reid.

All rights reserved. Published by Scholastic Inc., 557 Broadway, New York, NY 10012 by arrangement with Macmillan Children's Books, a division of Macmillan Publishers Ltd.

SCHOLASTIC and associated logos are trademarks and/or registered trademarks of Scholastic Inc.

12 11 10 9 8 7 6 5 4   4 5 6 7/0

Printed in the U.S.A.   40
First Scholastic printing, April 2002

SPECIAL THANKS TO NARINDER DHAMI

CHAPTER ONE

"Jake! Come here!"

Neil Parker dashed after his excitable black and-white puppy. But he was too late. Jake had spotted a jump rope, and he eagerly grabbed one end of it. He began to shake it from side to side, growling. Neil felt a blush creeping into his cheeks as everyone else in the barn began to laugh. All the other dogs that were there with their owners for a Sunday morning training session started to get excited, too. Chaos was in the air.

"He thinks it's a snake!" Neil's little sister, Sarah, giggled. "Stop it, Jake!" She tried to pull the rope free, but Jake hung on determinedly.

"I didn't know you were going to teach Jake how to

attack ropes, Dad!" Emily, Neil's nine-year-old sister, remarked with a grin.

"He's pretty good at that already!" Bob Parker said with a smile.

Neil's parents, Bob and Carole, ran King Street Kennels, a boarding kennel and rescue center just outside the small country town of Compton. Bob also held regular twice-weekly training sessions for local people and their dogs in Red's Barn, which was next to the kennel blocks behind the Parkers' house. Neil loved his life with the dogs at King Street, and he couldn't imagine ever wanting to live anywhere else.

"Come on, trouble!" Neil scooped Jake up into his

arms, and the Border collie immediately let go of the rope so that he could lick Neil's nose. "You're going to start learning how to behave yourself so you can be just like your dad."

Sam, Neil's black-and-white collie, wagged his tail excitedly, his eyes bright and alert. Neil gently ruffled the older collie's ears. He was always careful to show Sam as much attention as possible whenever Jake was around, even though Sam had shown no signs of being jealous of his son. Jake was a miniature version of Sam — they both had the same silky coats and shiny black noses.

"Ready to try again?" Bob asked, smiling.

Neil told Sam to sit. Sam immediately did so, and Neil couldn't help feeling proud of the way the collie responded to him. Sam was a fantastic dog. Neil had spent most of his free time training him to take part in agility competitions. But when Sam had collapsed at the end of a competition, Neil's life changed. Sam had a heart murmur, and Neil knew that his beloved dog was living on borrowed time.

"I hope you're watching this, Jake!" Neil said to the wriggling puppy in his arms. "Because you've got a lot to live up to!"

But before the session could get started, there was another interruption. Carole Parker, Neil's mother, popped her head into the doorway of the barn.

"Bob? There's a phone call for you."

Neil looked up, surprised at the tone of his mother's

voice. Carole, tall and dark-haired, was usually un-flappable, even in a crisis. But right now she looked pale and sounded nervous.

"Well . . ." Bob glanced around the barn. Eight people and their dogs, plus Neil and Jake, were wait-ing for the training session to begin. "Can't it wait?"

Carole shook her head. "It's urgent."

Bob frowned. "OK. I'm on my way." He turned back to the owners and their pets. "Sorry. I won't be long. While you're waiting, try those sit-and-stay tech-niques we practiced last week."

"What do you think that's all about?" Emily said in a low voice to Neil as Bob hurried out.

Neil shrugged. "I'm not sure. Mom looked a little wound up, didn't she?"

"Maybe it's just because the kennels are almost full," Emily suggested. "You know how busy we get at the beginning of vacation time, and Kate's not here this week."

Neil grinned and nodded. School vacations were always King Street's busiest times of the year, and their kennel assistant, Kate McGuire, was on vaca-tion herself at the moment.

"What are you going to do?" Sarah asked as Neil put Jake down on the floor.

"Teach him to sit," Neil replied confidently.

Emily and Sarah grinned. Jake was now dancing around Neil's feet, trying to pull the laces out of his sneakers.

"You'll have to get him to stand still first!" Emily pointed out.

"That's what these are for." Neil took out a packet of the dog treats he always carried. "You wait, by the end of this vacation Jake'll be on his way to being as well behaved as Sam — *ow!*"

Jake had pounced on the trailing end of one of the shoelaces and had accidentally dug his claws into Neil's ankle. Emily and Sarah burst out laughing.

"You mean the vacation *next* year, don't you?" Emily asked wickedly.

"Ha-ha. Very funny." Neil made a face at her. "Let's get started, Jake." He showed the puppy a dog treat, and Jake immediately looked interested. Keeping the reward in view, Neil raised his hand slightly above the puppy's black nose.

"What are you doing?" Sarah asked curiously.

"Watch." Neil held his hand a little higher, and Jake, who was staring eagerly at the food, raised his head higher, too. As he did so, his chubby little bottom hit the ground.

"Good boy!" Neil said quickly, and gave the puppy the treat. Jake swallowed it greedily. Then Neil repeated the action, not giving Jake another treat until the puppy's bottom was firmly on the floor.

"See?" He turned to Sarah and Emily. "In a little while Jake will sit whenever I raise my hand, whether I give him a treat or not."

"Neil?" Carole looked through the doorway of

Red's Barn again and beckoned to him, her face excited. "Quick! Your dad wants to see you and the girls in the office!"

"Why?" Neil asked curiously, but his mother had already disappeared.

"Something really weird's going on!" Emily said as Neil picked Jake up. "I wonder what happened."

"Well, we won't find out by standing here!" Neil said, giving Emily a push. "Come on!"

They all hurried outside, Sam at their heels, Jake in Neil's arms, and headed for the office, which was built onto the side of the Parkers' house.

Bob Parker was sitting in front of the King Street Kennels computer, looking slightly dazed, while Carole was perched on the desk, her eyes shining. They both smiled widely as Neil, Emily, and Sarah rushed in.

"Don't look so worried!" Bob told them, swiveling around to face them. "I've got some good news for you!"

"What's going on?" Neil asked curiously as he put Jake down on the floor. The puppy immediately went off to explore underneath the desk, but Sam stayed close to Neil's side, his doggy instincts obviously telling him that something important was happening.

Bob took a deep breath. "A lawyer in Melbourne, Australia, has just called to tell me that my great-aunt Victoria has died."

"*Who?*" Neil, Emily, and Sarah said together.

"Great-aunt Victoria, my grandfather's sister," Bob

explained. "She emigrated to Australia years ago, when I was just a boy."

"You've never mentioned her, Dad," Neil said, fondling Sam's silky head.

"Well, to be honest, she didn't really get along with the rest of the family," Bob explained, sitting Sarah on his knee. "So after she moved to Australia, she didn't keep in touch."

"Were they asking you to go over for the funeral?" Emily asked.

Bob shook his head. "No, the funeral's already taken place, but they've been trying to trace me for the last few weeks. They needed to contact me because" — he took another deep breath — "Great-aunt Victoria left me some money in her will. Quite a lot of money, actually."

Neil's eyes opened wide. "How much, Dad?"

"Well" — Bob cleared his throat — "ninety-eight thousand pounds, to be exact."

"Ninety-eight thousand pounds?" Neil and Emily repeated in stunned voices.

"We're rich!" Sarah squealed, bouncing up and down on her father's knee.

Neil and Emily stared at each other, their mouths open in amazement. Ninety-eight thousand pounds? Neil couldn't even imagine what a quarter of that amount of money would look like. "It's like winning the lottery!" he cried.

"What are you going to do with it all, Dad?" Emily asked, her eyes wide like saucers.

"Give me a chance to get used to it first!" Bob glanced at Carole. "You can see why I was so shocked. I didn't have a clue that Great-aunt Victoria would leave me anything."

"Daddy, can I have another hamster?" Sarah piped up again. "Fudge needs a friend!"

Bob laughed. "We'll have to see, sweetheart."

"I still can't believe it!" Carole exclaimed, her face breaking into a smile. "Ninety-eight thousand pounds! Thank you, Great-aunt Victoria!"

"It's a shame the lawyers couldn't get in touch in time for me to go to the funeral," Bob said soberly. "I don't suppose any of the family was there."

Neil wondered what it was like to move thousands of miles away from your family and never see them again. He couldn't help feeling sorry for his dad's great-aunt Victoria. "I wonder why she left the money to you, Dad?" he said.

Bob smiled. "The attorney said it was because of Winston. He was Victoria's dog. I used to take him for walks before they left for Australia. The lawyer said that she'd never forgotten that."

"Dad, what are you going to do with all the money?" Emily repeated impatiently.

"I don't have any idea." Bob looked at Carole. "We'll have to talk it over and decide a few things."

"We could have a swimming pool!" Emily suggested, her eyes shining.

"One pool for us, and another for the dogs!" Neil added. "Dad, you could build more kennel blocks so we can take in more dogs! And you could expand the rescue center, and —"

"Hang on a minute!" Bob held up a hand. "Don't get carried away! We need to think about all this carefully."

"Yes, we might be a lot richer than we were ten minutes ago, but we've still got a crowd of dogs waiting to be trained in the barn, plus there's only one empty cage left in the kennel!" Carole added with a twinkle in her eye. "So it's all hands on deck!"

"This is amazing!" Emily said happily to Neil as they went across the courtyard to Kennel Block One. "We're rich — we can buy anything we want!"

"I know," Neil agreed. He was already imagining all the extra dogs King Street Kennels would be able to help.

"Did you say *ninety-eight thousand pounds*?" Chris Wilson stared at Neil, with his mouth open.

Neil grinned at the look on his best friend's face. "Yep. Cool, isn't it?"

It was the following morning, and Neil had taken Sam and Jake for a quick walk in the surrounding fields. On their way home, they had met Chris, who was on his way to King Street. Neil had wasted no time in giving his friend the amazing news about Great-aunt Victoria's legacy. His mom and dad hadn't really wanted anyone outside the family to know about it at first, but Sarah hadn't been able to keep quiet and was telling everyone she met, so now the secret was out anyway.

"You lucky dog!" Chris said enviously. "What is the Puppy Patrol going to *do* with all that cash?" Neil and his family were used to being called the Puppy Patrol. The nickname had come about because they were seen around Compton so often in their Range Rover with the King Street logo on the side.

"Well, it's Dad's money, not mine." Neil turned to check on Sam and Jake, who were sniffing around in the hedges.

"So what *is* your dad going to do with it?" Chris went on.

Neil frowned. "I'm not sure. I think he's still getting used to the idea. He and Mom have been talking about it nonstop since yesterday morning."

"I bet I know what you want to do." Chris grinned. "You want to make King Street Kennels ten times bigger!"

Neil grinned back. "Well, why not?" he said as they arrived back at King Street. "I can't think of a better way to spend Great-aunt Victoria's money than on dogs!"

Neil unlocked the front door, and Jake charged in first, pelting full speed down the hall toward the kitchen. Sam followed at a more relaxed pace, and Neil checked, as he always did, that the older dog hadn't gotten too tired. But he seemed fine.

"Well, I don't think we can decide anything just yet, Bob." Neil glanced up at the sound of his mother's voice. She was on the landing overhead, with his father. "We've got to think this through carefully."

"I agree," Bob Parker said in a low voice. "But we're going to have to tell the kids what we're considering as soon as possible. They're involved in this as much as we are."

"I know," Carole replied softly, "I'm just not looking forward to it very much, that's all." She stopped abruptly when she caught sight of Neil and Chris in the hall below. "Hello, boys. I didn't hear you come in."

"I met Chris on my way back from walking the dogs," Neil said, staring hard at his parents. Both of them looked tired and strained, and they certainly didn't look like two people who'd just inherited an enormous sum of money. He couldn't help wondering what his mom had meant when she'd said she wasn't "looking forward to" telling the kids. He didn't like the sound of that at all. Telling them *what*?

At that moment Emily and Sarah appeared in the kitchen doorway.

"Chris, we're rich!" Sarah told him breathlessly. "We're millionaires!"

"Not quite, Squirt," Emily said. "You need a million pounds to be a millionaire."

"Well, we've got lots, anyway!" Sarah informed Chris. She grabbed his hand. "Come upstairs and see Fudge! I'm teaching him to play checkers!"

Chris raised his eyebrows. "This I've got to see!"

He followed Sarah upstairs, and Neil went into the kitchen, where Jake and Sam were waiting patiently by their empty bowls. As Neil gave his dogs some food, he couldn't help worrying about what he'd overheard. What on earth was going on? He was about to ask Emily if she knew anything when their father came into the kitchen.

"Your mom and I would like to talk to you and Emily, Neil," he said quietly.

Neil frowned as Carole hurried in, too, closing the door behind her. "What about?" he asked warily.

"About what we're going to do with Great-aunt Victoria's money," Bob said. There was a brief pause, then he went on. "Obviously, it's wonderful to be handed thousands of pounds out of the blue, but we do need to discuss exactly how we're going to spend it." He paused again, looking from Neil to Emily. "And it might mean a few changes in our lifestyle."

"Changes?" Neil repeated, his insides churning.

Carole nodded. "We haven't made up our minds one way or another yet."

"But we think it's only fair to discuss it with you two first," Bob continued. "Because one of the options we have to consider is selling King Street Kennels and moving."

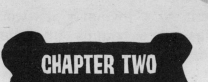

CHAPTER TWO

Neil stood as still as stone, feeling as if he'd been punched very hard right in his stomach. He couldn't believe what he'd just heard. His parents were thinking of selling King Street Kennels? How could they even *consider* it? He glanced at Emily, seeing the shock on her face.

"You don't mean it," Neil said in a shaky voice. "You wouldn't sell King Street Kennels. You *couldn't*."

"Neil, we didn't say we were *going* to." His mother rushed to reassure him. "It's just one of many things we've got to consider."

"Why?" Emily demanded, almost in tears. "We're happy here! We don't want to live anywhere else!"

Neil could feel himself shaking all over. He couldn't imagine life without King Street Kennels and all the dogs that passed through as boarders or as strays — and he'd always thought his parents felt exactly the same way. Obviously, though, they didn't.

"I don't understand," Neil muttered, staring at his father. "I thought you loved the dogs."

Bob sighed. "Neil, we do. Nobody could do this job if they didn't love dogs. But it's backbreaking work, you know that."

"The money's given us the option to think about doing something different," Carole went on gently. "We're not saying we're *going* to sell — just that we have to think about it very carefully."

"Basically we've got three options," Bob continued. "We can keep going as we are, maybe with some extra help so that we can take it a little easier. Or we can use the money to expand King Street. Or we can sell and do something different."

"But where would we go?" Emily asked miserably. "Would we have to leave Compton?"

"Emily, we haven't gotten that far yet," Bob said quietly. "Ninety-eight thousand pounds might *seem* like a lot of money, but it's not enough for your mom and me to retire on. We'll need to keep working. It just may not be at King Street."

"But it'll almost certainly still be with dogs, one way or another," Carole added, looking anxiously at Neil and Emily.

"When will you decide?" Neil asked, feeling as if his whole world had turned upside down.

"We're still discussing it," Bob replied. "But as soon as we've reached a decision, you'll be the first to know, I promise."

"What about Sarah?" Emily asked.

"We don't want Sarah to know until we've made up our minds one way or another," Carole said firmly. "And remember, even if we *do* decide to sell and leave, we'll still have Sam and Jake, and dogs will always be an enormous part of our lives."

But it wouldn't be the same, Neil thought. Nothing on earth could beat living at King Street. Nothing. Why couldn't his parents understand that?

He glanced at Emily and read the same determination in her eyes. Together, they would have to try to change their parents' minds if they decided to do the unthinkable and leave King Street Kennels.

"You look as bad as I feel," Neil whispered to Emily when they met on the landing the following morning. Neil had tossed and turned for hours the night before, his mind going over and over everything that his parents had said. Emily, too, looked pale and heavy-eyed.

"I can't stop thinking about what Mom and Dad said yesterday," Emily whispered. But she broke off abruptly as Sarah's bedroom door opened and the youngest Parker headed for the bathroom.

Neil hadn't felt like getting up early this morning, but he knew that Sam and Jake and the other dogs at the kennel would be expecting their morning walks. However bad he felt, he couldn't let the dogs down. But how many more mornings would he be getting up to help out with the King Street dogs? Not many, if his parents decided to leave.

Carole and Bob were already in the kitchen when Neil walked in. Sam and Jake immediately rushed over to greet him. It was early for visitors, so Neil was surprised to see his uncle sitting at the table.

"Hello, Neil." Jack Tansley, Carole's brother, gave him a friendly grin.

Neil frowned. "I thought you were supposed to be in London, Uncle Jack."

"Slight change of plans, Neil. Aunt Mary and

Steve have gone, but I've stayed behind." He glanced at Bob and Carole.

Neil felt sick inside. What was it now? He petted Sam and Jake gently, grateful for the dogs' warm, comforting presence.

"That's right, Neil. Your dad and I have decided to get away for a few days by ourselves. To think things through."

"We need to make a decision as quickly as possible," said Bob. "Jack has agreed to step in and take over."

Jack nodded. "I don't like London much, so I'm glad to have an excuse not to go! And I've run the kennel before, when you went to Cornwall. Remember?"

"Kate was here then," added Carole. "But she'll be back on Friday. You and Emily will give Jack a hand, won't you?"

"Sure we will!" Neil said eagerly. It was a huge strain, waiting to hear what decision his parents would make. If they went away for a while, it would ease the pressure on all of them. And maybe his parents would realize how much they would miss King Street if they moved.

"I'm just going to try to reserve somewhere to stay now." Bob was already heading for the phone. "Thanks, Jack. We really appreciate this."

After breakfast, things moved quickly. Within an hour, Bob had arranged for himself and Carole to spend a week in a cottage in the Scottish Highlands.

There were all the dogs to be fed and walked, then Neil and Emily helped their mother pack and also to pacify Sarah, who had burst into tears when she found out their parents were going away without them.

Just before midday, they were ready to leave. Bob came over to check on the rest of the family. "All set?"

Carole nodded, and everyone went outside, followed by Sam and Jake. Carole gave Sarah a big hug, then kissed Neil and Emily.

"Bye," she said quietly. "And don't worry. We'll tell you as soon as we've come to a decision."

Neil nodded, trying not to show how worried he was. Would it be good or bad news?

Bob hugged Sarah and Emily and squeezed Neil's shoulder. "I know you'll give your uncle Jack all the help he needs," he said. "See you next week."

Neil couldn't trust himself to speak. As his parents climbed into the car, he petted Sam, who was pressed reassuringly close against his side, sensing his distress. They all waved as the car pulled away and until it was out of sight.

"Well, let's go have some lunch," Jack suggested.

Before anyone could answer, another car pulled into the driveway. Mike Turner, the local vet, leaned out and grinned at them.

"Hi there. Bob asked me to stop by to see one of the dogs that has an eye infection."

"Yes, that's Robbie," Neil said. He pushed the

thought of his parents firmly out of his mind. All that mattered now was that the kennel was run properly and the dogs were kept safe and happy. Moping around wondering what his parents were deciding wouldn't help anyone.

"Right." Mike opened the car door and reached for his bag.

"Do you want a hand with your stuff?" Jack moved toward him. Unfortunately so did Jake, who had just stopped chasing his tail and was charging toward the vet's car, barking a welcome.

"Jake!" Neil yelled. "Uncle Jack, look out!"

Uncle Jack looked around just as the excited puppy tried to weave through his legs to get to Mike Turner. Jack was knocked off balance and fell to the ground, landing awkwardly on his arm.

"Uncle Jack!" Neil, Emily, and Sarah rushed over. Mike was already kneeling down, examining Jack's twisted arm.

"Don't try to move it, Jack," Mike said quickly. "I think it might be broken!"

"They're back!" Neil jumped up from the sofa as he saw the vet's car pulling into the driveway later that afternoon. Jake, who was lying next to Sam, jumped up, too. "Oh, no, you don't!" Neil said sternly, tucking the wriggling puppy firmly under his arm. "You've done enough damage for one day!"

After the accident, Mike Turner had driven Uncle

Jack to the local hospital to have his arm X-rayed. Uncle Jack had been in a great deal of pain, and if Mike hadn't been there, they would have had to call an ambulance. Mike had also refused to leave Neil, Emily, and Sarah at King Street on their own, so Neil had called Chris, and he and his mom had hurried over to stay with them.

"You'll have to call your parents and tell them what's happened, won't you?" Chris said to Neil as they all went outside.

Neil shook his head. "No way. They need this vacation to figure things out. Anyway, Em and I want to show Mom and Dad that we'll work hard to keep the kennel going. Then they'll realize how much we want to stay."

Chris nodded, looking serious. He was still reeling from the shock of discovering that the Parkers might be leaving King Street.

Uncle Jack climbed out of Mike Turner's car. He had a plaster cast on his arm, but Neil was glad to see that he wasn't looking quite so pale.

"Are you all right, Uncle Jack?" Emily asked anxiously.

"I've been better," Jack said dryly. He reached out and scratched Jake's head. "For a little fella, you've certainly caused a lot of damage, Jacob Parker!"

"Does it hurt?" Sarah asked sympathetically.

Jack made a face. "Yes, but the doctor gave me some painkillers to take."

"It's quite a bad break," Mike Turner said as they all went inside. "And I hate to say this, Neil, but I think you'd better call your parents and ask them to come back."

"No!" Neil and Emily said at the same time. Mike looked taken aback.

"Mom and Dad really need this time away," Neil explained quickly. "Em and I can manage."

"Here, I've still got one good hand, right?" said Uncle Jack indignantly as Mrs. Wilson handed him a cup of tea. "Between the three of us —"

"Four!" Sarah interrupted.

"Between the four of us, we can manage. And Kate's due back on Friday."

"But that's four days away." Mike frowned. "Are you sure you can manage until then?"

"I'll come over every day to help," offered Chris.

"And I could lend a hand with the cooking," Chris's mom added.

"Well, if you're sure." Mike shrugged.

Uncle Jack nodded. "We can manage."

Neil could tell that Mike had sensed there was something going on, but he wasn't going to pry.

"Well, I'll drop in as often as I can this week, too." Mike stood up. "Now I'd better take a look at Robbie's eye infection."

"Thanks, Mike," Neil said gratefully. He knew how busy the vet was, and he must have had to cancel some of his afternoon appointments to take Uncle

Jack to the hospital. Mrs. Wilson and Chris, too, were giving up their time to help them out. If they did move away from Compton, they would be leaving all these good, loyal friends behind.

"Phew! I never knew looking after the kennel was such hard work!" Chris staggered out of Kennel Block One carrying a pile of dog dishes. "I'm tired out from walking all those dogs!"

"Don't be a wimp!" Neil was behind him, carrying another load of dishes. "Come on, the dogs want their food!"

"So do I!" grumbled Emily, who joined them from Kennel Block Two, also loaded down with dog bowls. "I'm starving!"

Neil and Emily had only realized the extent of the task they'd taken on when evening came and it was time for all the dogs to be fed and walked. Uncle Jack had helped at first, but his arm had obviously been hurting, so he went inside to take a painkiller. Neil was extremely grateful that Chris was there to lend a hand.

"Look!" Chris stopped so suddenly that Neil almost ran into him. "What's the matter with your uncle?"

Uncle Jack was standing near the back door of the house, staring around him as if he couldn't remember where he was and swaying slightly from side to side.

Neil frowned. "It must be those painkillers the doctor gave him. Those pills can be pretty strong!"

He hurried over to his uncle. "Uncle Jack, are you all right?"

"What?" Jack stared at Neil blearily. "Yes, I'm fine."

"You don't look it." Neil guided him gently back into the house. "Why don't you go and lie down?"

"All right." Uncle Jack yawned hugely. "I *am* feeling a bit woozy."

"A bit woozy!" Chris repeated when Neil came back. "He was totally out of it!"

Emily looked worried. "Poor Uncle Jack. He's not going to be much use to us in that state, is he?"

"Mike Turner's definitely going to want you to call your parents now," Chris pointed out.

Neil looked defiant. "We'll just have to keep Uncle Jack out of everyone's way if he's taking those pills," he said in a determined voice. "All we've got to do is keep our heads down and play it cool, and we'll make it through until Friday, when Kate gets back."

Chris stared at him. "But that means we're going to be running the kennel on our own!" he gasped.

"Well, we can do it!" Emily said stubbornly.

"Yes, *of course* we can!" Neil agreed with more conviction than he really felt.

The telephone in the office rang just then, and Neil hurried over to answer it while Chris and Emily went to wash the dogs' bowls.

"Hello, King Street Kennels," he said politely, wondering if it would be his father. Bob had promised to call home as soon as they were settled in Scotland.

"Hello. My name is Rachel James, and I want to board a dog for one week, starting tomorrow," said a brisk voice. "Do you have room?"

Neil hesitated. Maybe he shouldn't take in any more animals with things as they were. But one more dog wasn't going to make that much difference, and they did have a pen available.

"Yes, we do."

"Good," Rachel James said, pleased. "The dog's name is Molly, and she's" — she paused — "yes, she's a terrier mix."

Neil frowned. Didn't Rachel James know what color and type her own dog was?

"We're open from nine-thirty, Ms. James, so you can bring your dog in anytime you like after that."

Rachel laughed. "Oh, Molly isn't *my* dog. She belongs to Kerry, my employer."

"Oh," said Neil. There was a pause, then Rachel James said sharply, "You *do* know who Molly is, don't you?"

"Yes, you just said she was a terrier mix," Neil said, even more puzzled by now.

"Don't you ever read the papers?" Rachel asked with a little laugh. "Pictures of Molly have been in the tabloids for the last few weeks!"

Neil frowned. He didn't read the newspapers much, but he usually took notice of any dog stories. Then slowly it began to dawn on him. He remembered Emily mentioning something about a famous dog.

"You mean — ?" he said faintly.

"Yes, Molly is Kerry Kirby's dog!" Rachel snapped. "You *have* heard of Kerry Kirby, haven't you?"

"Yes," Neil said weakly. Kerry Kirby was the lead singer of All Spice, Emily's favorite band. It was one of the most successful groups in the world! Kerry was in the news because she was dating a famous Liverpool soccer player, Michael Newman. It was Michael who'd adopted the dog from a rescue center in Liverpool and given her to Kerry just a few weeks ago. The media were already speculating wildly that Molly might be a secret engagement present and that the celebrity couple were planning to get married.

"All Spice is touring in the north for the next week or so," Rachel explained. "And Kerry wants Molly close by so she can pick her up at the end of the tour. We'll need to drop the dog off at about eight-thirty tomorrow morning because of our schedule. Is that all right with you?"

"Uh — yes." Neil was still too stunned to object.

"Kerry herself will be bringing Molly tomorrow," Rachel went on cheerfully. "So you can expect the press to be out in force — they'll want lots of pictures!"

Neil felt himself turn white. So much for keeping a low profile. Tomorrow one of the most famous dogs in the country would be moving into King Street Kennels, and if anything went wrong, the whole world would soon know about it.

CHAPTER THREE

"**I** can't believe it! Kerry Kirby and her dog are coming to King Street Kennels tomorrow!" Emily said ecstatically. "You could look a little more excited, Neil!"

"At any other time I would be," Neil said grimly. "But if anyone finds out we're running the kennel on our own, we're sunk."

Neil, Emily, and Chris were in the Parkers' living room. Sarah had bounded off to her bedroom to tell Fudge the exciting news, and Mrs. Wilson, who had come over with a casserole for dinner, was cleaning up the kitchen. Luckily, Uncle Jack was upstairs, fast asleep, while Chris's mom was in the house.

"But why should having Kerry Kirby's dog here make any difference?" Chris asked.

"Well, for one thing, Uncle Jack's got to be there to check the dog in," Neil said.

"I see what you mean." Chris nodded. "People will start getting suspicious if there are only kids around!"

Emily frowned. "So that means we've got to persuade Uncle Jack not to take any painkillers!"

"Exactly," Neil said. He could just see the headlines now: *Kids run kennel while uncle is down for the count!* He didn't know if his parents were bothering with newspapers up in the Scottish Highlands, but if they saw any stories like that, they'd race right home.

"We've got to make sure nothing goes wrong," he said urgently. "Because if it does, we'll be in big trouble."

The phone in the hall interrupted his thought.

"I bet that's Dad," Emily said nervously.

Neil went to answer it, his heart pounding. If it was his father, he would have to make sure he didn't give anything away.

"Hello, Neil?"

"Hello, Dad!" Neil hoped he sounded cheerful. "Did you have a good trip?"

"Yes, we arrived safely," Bob told him. "How's everything at home?"

"Fine," Neil said calmly. "Don't worry about anything here, Dad."

"Good. I'm calling from the nearest village, because the cottage doesn't have a phone. If you need to contact us, you can leave a message with the owner, Mrs. MacDonald." Bob gave Neil the number. "Is Jack around?"

Neil gulped. "No, he's out with some of the dogs."

"OK, I'll speak to him next time I call. Give my love to the girls."

Neil couldn't help feeling guilty as he hung up, but he hadn't *really* lied. All the dogs had been fed and walked, despite Uncle Jack's injury, so everything *was* fine. He just hoped things would stay that way when Kerry Kirby and Molly arrived tomorrow.

"Look at all those photographers!" Emily gasped, staring through the living-room window the following morning. "And more are coming!"

"Maybe they'll want to photograph us, too!" Sarah said, her eyes as round as saucers.

Neil joined his sisters at the window. There were five photographers hanging around outside King Street already, all loaded down with cameras and flashes, and a couple more cars were pulling up at the side of the road. Emily nudged Neil.

"There's Jake Fielding." Jake was a photographer with the local *Compton News* and had often covered stories about King Street dogs.

Neil glanced at the clock. "I'd better go and wake Uncle Jack up."

"And don't let him take any painkillers!" Emily reminded him.

Just as Neil was about to go upstairs, the doorbell rang. He opened the front door cautiously, thinking it might be one of the photographers, but it was Chris, along with Hasheem Lindon, their friend from school, and Emily's friend Julie. They all looked very excited.

"Have you seen the photographers?" they said together.

Neil nodded as he let them in. He and Emily had called Hasheem and Julie the day before, and they'd both offered to come over and help out when they heard about Uncle Jack's accident. Neil was hoping that the day would run smoothly with so many helpful hands around. Once they'd gotten over the tricky business of checking in a pop star's dog, of course.

"Em and Sarah are watching for Kerry and Molly to arrive." Neil headed for the stairs. "I've got to wake Uncle Jack — he's still snoring his head off!"

But Neil was in for a shock. When he went into the guest bedroom, Jack was already up and dressed.

"Morning, Uncle Jack." Neil glanced anxiously at the bottle of painkillers on the bedside cabinet. Had his uncle taken one yet or not? "How's your arm?"

Jack grimaced. "It still hurts. I had a good night's sleep, though." He frowned. "I don't remember much about yesterday. Did we get all the dogs fed and walked last night?"

"Yes, we did," Neil assured him. "Do you think you'll need to take any of those pills today?"

"Oh, I've just taken a couple," Uncle Jack said. "I can't manage without them yet."

Neil's heart plummeted. That meant they only had about twenty minutes before Uncle Jack started getting woozy again.

"Neil!" That was Emily, shrieking at the top of her voice. "They're here!"

Neil looked out the bedroom window. A white Mercedes was pulling into the driveway, and the photographers were eagerly surrounding it.

"Who's here?" Uncle Jack asked, puzzled.

Neil quickly explained as he hurried his uncle downstairs.

"Oh. I don't remember taking the call yesterday," Uncle Jack remarked, still puzzled.

"You didn't, I did," Neil told him.

"That's pretty exciting, looking after a pop star's dog, isn't it!" Uncle Jack said. Then to Neil's dismay, he yawned widely. "Oh, dear, must be those painkillers that're making me drowsy."

Neil's heart began to thump nervously. *Please stay awake long enough to check Molly in, Uncle Jack,* he thought.

Emily and the others were already waiting in the driveway, their eyes popping out of their heads. The Mercedes drew smoothly to a halt, and a slim red-headed woman got out, followed by a burly bodyguard.

"Hello. Who's in charge here?" the woman asked briskly.

Uncle Jack hurried forward. "I am. Welcome to King Street Kennels."

"I'm Rachel James." She frowned. "You're not the person I spoke to yesterday."

"That was me," Neil said, conscious of all the photographers around them.

"Oh, right." Rachel glanced at the plaster cast on Uncle Jack's arm. "You look like you've been in a war. Are you sure you're well enough to look after Molly properly?"

Neil felt a thrill of horror run down his spine. "Of course we can," he assured her quickly.

"Great!" said a familiar voice, and Kerry Kirby climbed out of the Mercedes. She wore a zebra-print miniskirt and big platform shoes, and her hair was in dreadlocks. In the last All Spice video, her hair had been long and jet-black.

"Kerry, over here!" All the photographers started snapping away immediately. "Give us a smile, Kerry!"

Kerry grinned and waved at them. Then she reached into the car and picked up her dog.

"And this is Molly!" she told Neil and the others. Then she turned to pose for the photographers, who began firing off shots as fast as possible.

Neil inspected Molly more closely. She was small and sturdily built, with a golden-brown shaggy coat. She had the typical lively, alert look of a terrier. Her big brown eyes were full of interest as she stared at the photographers. She barked loudly every time a flash went off. Neil couldn't help smiling when he saw that the dog was wearing a red velvet collar and a large gold ID tag.

"Can we have one of the kennel kids in the picture?" Jake Fielding called out. "Come on, Neil, what about you?"

Neil turned pink.

"Yeah, go on, Neil!" Emily said eagerly.

Feeling embarrassed, Neil went over to stand next to Kerry Kirby. Molly immediately leaned toward him, barking with delight and sniffing Neil's scent. Neil put out his hand, and Molly licked it enthusi-

astically, pawing at his shoulder as the cameras clicked away. She was one of the liveliest dogs he'd ever met.

"That's all, folks," Rachel called, ushering Kerry and Molly away. "Jeff, will you bring Molly's things in?" The bodyguard immediately went to open the trunk, and Rachel turned to Uncle Jack. "Can we get Molly settled in quickly, please?"

"Of course," he said politely, stifling a yawn. Neil's heart began to thump nervously. He just hoped Uncle Jack wouldn't fall asleep in the middle of checking Molly in!

Uncle Jack led Kerry, Molly, and Rachel into the office, and Neil and the others crowded inside, too.

"There seem to be a lot of you!" Kerry remarked, raising her eyebrows. "Surely you don't *all* live here?"

"Our friends like to come and help out," Neil explained quickly. The others all seemed tongue-tied, especially Emily, who was staring at Kerry Kirby as if she couldn't believe she was really there. Only Sarah didn't seem fazed by the pop star's presence.

"My sister's got all your CDs," she told Kerry Kirby. "But she won't let me borrow them!"

"Sarah!" Emily hissed, mortified, but Kerry Kirby laughed.

"We *are* in a hurry, so could we make this as fast as possible?" Rachel glanced impatiently at Uncle Jack.

Neil kept a sharp eye on his uncle while he was entering Molly's details into the computer, but fortunately Uncle Jack managed to do everything correctly. Meanwhile the bodyguard had brought Molly's things into the office.

"These are her toys." Kerry pointed at a duffel bag bulging with rubber bones and Frisbees. Next to it was a basket lined with soft blankets and velvet cushions. "Molly *can* have her own basket in her pen, can't she?"

"Yes, of course." Neil stared at a pile of gold dog dishes that had MOLLY engraved on them. "What does she eat?"

"Chicken's her favorite," Kerry said. "There should be enough frozen meat here for her whole stay, but if you need more, just add it to my bill. Oh, and Molly likes to have this with her." Kerry held up a large, gold-framed publicity photograph of herself. "Can you put it in her pen?"

"Sure." Neil tried not to smile. He'd never seen a more pampered dog!

Kerry hugged Molly. "Be a good girl for your mom, won't you?" She turned to Neil. "She's very well behaved."

Molly barked and began chewing Kerry's dreadlocks.

"Would you like to have a look at the kennel?" Neil asked. Most owners wanted to check that the place where they were leaving their pet for the first time was clean and well kept.

Kerry hesitated.

"Kerry," Rachel James said urgently, "we really have to go."

"No, that's all right," Kerry told Neil. "King Street was recommended to me by a friend of mine, anyway. Jeff Calton — he produces *The Time Travelers*."

"Oh." Neil remembered Jeff. When his favorite TV show, *The Time Travelers*, had come to Padsham Castle to film on location, he and some of his friends had been cast as extras. It was good to know that Jeff remembered him and King Street Kennels.

Kerry hugged Molly again, then handed her over to Neil. "Look after her, won't you?" she said with a shaky smile, and hurried out with Rachel. Cameras clicked again as they got into their car.

"She's nice, isn't she?" Emily sighed as they all crowded around the window to watch the Mercedes pull away. The photographers began to drift away, too. "And she's crazy about Molly."

"You know what? I bet this dog's the poshest pup in England!" Hasheem said with a grin.

"And the silliest!" Neil groaned, trying to stop Molly from licking his ear off.

"Who's snoring?" Sarah asked.

They all turned around. Jack had dozed off, and his head was on the computer keyboard.

"I thought you were going to stop him from taking any painkillers, Neil!" Chris said.

"I didn't quite make it!" Neil sighed, leaning over to shake his uncle's shoulder. "Why don't you go back to the house and take a nap, Uncle Jack?"

"Eh?" Uncle Jack said, dazed. "Is it time for bed?"

"Yes, it is," Neil assured him. Uncle Jack yawned and staggered out.

"That was close," Emily said. "Another minute and he'd have fallen asleep in front of Kerry Kirby!"

"Yeah, that would have been *great* publicity for the kennel!" Neil groaned. "Let's go get Molly settled in. We've still got all the morning chores to do. And Mike said he would stop by. Everything has to look normal."

He set Molly down, intending to put her leash on. But as soon as the dog's paws touched the ground, she bolted toward the back door, which Uncle Jack had left open.

"Molly!" Neil yelled. "Come back!"

Molly just ran out into the backyard, snuffling eagerly around, her eyes darting everywhere. As Neil and the others raced after her, she easily dodged them, racing around at top speed.

"This is all we need!" Neil groaned as they chased after her. He had nightmare visions of another newspaper headline: *Incompetent kennel loses pop star's dog*.

"I thought she was supposed to be well behaved!" Chris gasped.

Just then Jake trotted out of the kitchen door. He

took one look at Molly and charged over to her, tail wagging furiously.

Molly eyed Jake with interest. While the two dogs were sniffing each other, Neil and Emily sidled over and managed to clip Molly's leash to her collar. Molly immediately grabbed it in her teeth, shaking it from side to side and growling playfully.

"Phew!" Neil gasped. "I think we've taken on a whole lot of trouble here!"

CHAPTER FOUR

"**H**ey, Em!" Neil said indignantly as he stuck his head into the office. His sister was sitting in front of the computer. "Come on, I need some help locking up the kennel for the night!"

"Sorry." Emily looked up as Neil came in, followed by Jake. "I was just checking some of the All Spice websites to see if I could find anything about Molly."

"Good idea!" Neil went into the office and looked at the computer screen. "Did you find anything?"

"There's some stuff here and there, but this one's the best." Emily clicked the mouse and accessed a site that had the title *The Molly Zone!* After a few seconds, a large picture of Molly appeared, too.

Neil grinned. "You mean there's a site that's just about Molly?"

Emily nodded. "Some nutty All Spice fans must have put it together. Look, it's got lots of information about Molly on it."

Neil scanned the screen. "'Molly's two years old, and she's a terrier mix,'" he read aloud. "'No one knows where Molly came from. Three months ago, she was left tied to the railing of a dog shelter in Liverpool. Then she was adopted by the soccer star Michael Newman and given to his girlfriend, Kerry Kirby of All Spice.'"

"How could someone have treated Molly like that!" Emily exclaimed angrily.

Neil nodded. No matter how many neglected or abandoned dogs he saw, it always shocked him that anyone could hurt a dog. His own dog, Sam, had been an abandoned puppy when he first came to King Street.

"It's amazing that she still trusts humans after what she's been through," said Neil. Jake was standing on his hind legs, trying to climb onto the desk to see what was going on, so Neil picked him up. "What else is there, Em?"

"This looks interesting!" Emily pointed to a section entitled "Amazing Facts About Molly." "'Molly's got twenty different collars,'" she read. "'Her favorite is a gold one with silver tassels on it!'"

"She probably likes chewing the tassels!" Neil remarked with a smile. "How do they know all this stuff, anyway?"

"I've seen some of these stories before, so I suppose they've copied them out of the newspapers." Emily skimmed down a list of "Amazing Facts" and read aloud: "'Molly once chewed up a pair of Kerry's designer shoes, which cost five hundred pounds!'"

Neil laughed. "I wonder why Kerry told us Molly was well behaved? She obviously isn't!"

"Maybe she thought we wouldn't take her if we knew the truth!" Emily pointed at the screen. "Check this out! 'Molly has her own playroom in Kerry's mansion in London, complete with an intercom, so that she can bark for the housekeeper when she wants her lunch!'" Emily logged off the computer. "It must be a drag for her, staying at King Street Kennels!" She giggled.

"She doesn't seem to mind!" Neil said. "Come on, let's go lock up, and we'll take Jake in to see her."

"Yeah, they certainly seem to like each other!" Emily commented as she, Neil, and Jake went to Kennel Block One.

"That's probably because Molly came from a shelter, so she's used to lots of other dogs being around," Neil pointed out. They went into the kennel block, and as they made their way down the aisle toward Molly's pen, he and Emily checked that the dogs were all safely locked in. Most of them were asleep, although some of them looked up sleepily as Neil, Emily, and Jake went by.

"I'm worried about Daisy." Emily stopped by a pen

that had a little white poodle in it. "She seems a bit off."

"She's not sick, is she?" Neil asked, alarmed.

"I think she just misses her owner," Emily said. "She's never been to a kennel before."

Daisy was lying in her basket, but she wasn't asleep. She stared mournfully at Neil with her big dark eyes, but she didn't move, not even when he held a dog treat through the wire mesh.

"We'll have to keep an eye on her," Neil said, worried, as they went over to Molly's pen. He was always concerned when dogs didn't settle in well at the kennel, but since he felt that he was in charge at the moment, it was up to him to make sure Daisy was happy. It was a big responsibility.

Molly, unsurprisingly, wasn't asleep. When Neil, Emily, and Jake went into the pen, she hurled herself at them joyfully.

"She's a handful, isn't she?" said Emily as Molly and Jake ran around each other in circles, nipping affectionately at each other's tails.

"Yeah, she's pretty crazy!" Neil said. "I guess the kind of lifestyle she leads doesn't help, either. Kerry's away from home a lot, so I suppose Molly travels around with her most of the time."

Emily nodded. "I imagine that Molly hasn't really had a chance to settle down in one place."

"*And* she's got tons of energy!" Neil petted Molly's head, then was nearly knocked over backward when

Molly launched herself at him enthusiastically. "No wonder she gets overexcited. Did you see her with Mike earlier? She nearly licked him to death!"

"How was Uncle Jack when Mike came by?" Emily asked anxiously.

"He was all right," Neil said thankfully. "The pain-killers he'd taken this morning had almost worn off by then. And I told Mike the real reason why Mom and Dad are away."

"What did he say?"

"He was shocked," Neil admitted. "But at least it took his mind off Uncle Jack's yawning!"

Emily grinned. "So we're still managing to get away with it?"

"Just about. And maybe Uncle Jack won't need to take those pills for too much longer." Molly pounced playfully on Jake again, and Neil smiled. "I think I'd better take Molly for a really long walk tomorrow morning and tire her out a bit!" He looked thoughtful. "Maybe I'll include her in Jake's training sessions, too."

Emily glanced at the photo of Kerry Kirby, hanging in one corner of the pen. "Do you think Kerry would mind?"

"I don't think so. It must be difficult taking Molly around with her if the dog's not trained." Neil looked determined. "Anyway, it can't hurt."

Emily shrugged and yawned.

"You're as bad as Uncle Jack!" Neil teased her.

"I'm really tired," Emily complained. "And we haven't finished feeding all the dogs yet."

"I know." Neil was suddenly conscious of his own exhaustion. Hasheem, Chris, and Julie had helped out with all the feeding and walking of the dogs that day, but there had been plenty of other things happening, too. People had been calling to make reservations for their pets for the next few months; a van had arrived with a delivery of dog food, which Neil had had to take charge of and check carefully; and Robbie's eye infection had suddenly gotten worse. Neil had always known that running the kennel was hard work, but now he really got it. He was beginning to understand why his parents might be considering changing their lifestyle. Even if they could afford extra help, life at the kennel would never be easy. "I wonder how Mom and Dad are doing?"

"Well, they couldn't have decided anything yet or they would've called. It seems like years to wait until they get back next Tuesday, doesn't it?"

"It seems like years to wait until *Friday*, when Kate gets back," Neil pointed out. Once Kate returned, things would be a lot easier. But there was still another long, hard day to get through before that would happen.

Neil forced himself to open his eyes, then blinked in the sunlight that was streaming into his bedroom. He had been woken up by the noise of barking. He was so used to hearing the dogs that it usually didn't bother him, but now it sounded as if they were all barking at once. He checked the time. A quarter to nine! He should have been up more than an hour ago to start the morning walks! Groaning, Neil rolled out of bed and grabbed his jeans. As he hurried out onto the landing, pulling his sweatshirt over his head, he bumped into Emily, who was dashing downstairs, too.

"We're late!" she gasped. "All the dogs are going crazy!"

"I know!" Neil's voice was muffled as he fought to get his sweatshirt on. "Are Uncle Jack and Sarah up?"

"Sarah is," Emily replied. "Uncle Jack's still asleep."

"We'd better take Sarah with us," Neil decided.

"She can walk Barney, the little Yorkie. I'll take Molly and Jake. You take Scooter the Labrador and Daisy — it might cheer her up a little. We'll give the other dogs a run in the exercise field when we get back."

Neil hurried into the living room, where Sarah was stretched out on the carpet, watching a cartoon. "Come on, Squirt! We need you to help with walking the dogs!"

Sarah jumped up eagerly. "Can I walk Molly?"

"We'll see," Neil said vaguely. He had no intention of letting anyone except himself handle Molly — she was such a handful.

"Have you seen all those people outside?" Sarah asked as she followed him out, but Neil wasn't listening. He went into the kitchen to get Jake, who was curled up under the table next to his father. Both dogs jumped to their feet when Neil came in, and they rushed up to fuss over him as if they hadn't seen him for days. Neil clipped Jake's leash to his collar and shook his head gently at Sam, who was staring up at him hopefully.

"Not today, boy," he said, petting the collie's silky ears. "We're going for a *long* walk. I'll take you into the field when I get back, OK?"

"Emily, did you *see* all those people outside?" Sarah asked impatiently when Emily arrived at the back door with Daisy and Barney and a black Labrador named Scooter. But Emily wasn't listening, either.

"Molly's up and running around her pen already!"
Emily grinned at Neil. "I think you're going to have
to walk to London and back to tire that one out!"

"Or maybe I should just give her one of Uncle
Jack's painkillers!" Neil said as he headed toward
Kennel Block One. "By the way, Em, you'd better
leave a note for him to say where we've gone."

Molly was amusing herself by dragging all the
cushions out of her basket. She stopped as soon as
she saw Neil and started whining and pawing at the
pen door.

"Good girl!" Neil clipped the leash firmly to her
collar. "Let's go for a walk, OK?"

Molly barked gleefully and dragged Neil along, almost pulling his arm from its socket. For a small dog,
she was strong, and she rushed Neil across the
courtyard to where Emily and Sarah were waiting
with the other dogs. Molly sniffed them all in a
friendly way, but she went nuts with joy when she
saw Jake.

"They love each other!" Sarah said, delighted.

"Maybe we should suggest to Kerry that she get
another dog to keep Molly company," Neil said as
they all went to the front of the house.

"You can't tell *Kerry Kirby* of All Spice what to do!"
Emily gasped, scandalized.

"Why not?" Neil shrugged. "If it means Molly will
be happier, she should be pleased."

A bark behind him made him look around. Sam was trotting toward them, looking very pleased with himself. Neil groaned.

"Oh, no, how did *he* get out? Go home, Sam! Home!"

"Neil!" Emily suddenly nudged him hard in the ribs. "Look!"

Neil turned around, and his eyes widened in amazement. There was a crowd of about fifteen people standing on the driveway in front of the house. Most of them were teenagers, and they were wearing All Spice T-shirts and pins and carrying All Spice banners.

"See?" Sarah piped up triumphantly. "I *told* you there were people standing outside!"

"What're they doing?" Emily whispered to Neil, but before he had a chance to say anything, one of the girls in the crowd saw them.

"That's Kerry's dog!" she shouted, and Neil's heart began to race with fear as everyone rushed toward them. Before they could move, he, Emily, and Sarah were surrounded by excited people, all fighting to try to pet Molly.

"Get out of the way — please!" Neil yelled, feeling really scared as the crowd of fans pressed in on them. He could hear Sam barking frantically, although he couldn't see the collie. "You're frightening the dogs!"

Jake was cowering against Neil's legs, terrified. Molly thought this was all great fun and barked loudly, jumping around and getting tangled up in her leash. Meanwhile, Sam, knowing from the tone of his voice that Neil was upset, was running desperately around the edge of the crowd, trying to get to his master. Neil could hear the collie's barking becoming hoarser, as if he was coughing. Emily looked pale and scared, and Neil couldn't even see Sarah and Barney. He looked around for help, and miraculously, it came.

"What on earth is going on here!" thundered a loud voice. Everyone fell silent, even the excited All Spice fans, as Uncle Jack strode out of the house, put his good arm around Sarah, who was crying, and glared at them. "This is private property, and you're trespassing!"

"We just wanted to see Kerry's dog," muttered a couple of the fans sheepishly.

"And now that you've seen her, I think you'd better go." Uncle Jack fixed the fans with a beady stare as they trailed away down the driveway, looking embarrassed.

"Thanks, Uncle Jack," Neil said gratefully, picking Jake up. The puppy still looked scared to death, although Molly was taking it in her stride, as usual. He glanced around, worried about Sam. "Is Sam OK?"

"Neil!" Emily's anguished shout made Neil spin around. What he saw made his heart turn over sickeningly in his chest.

"Sam!"

Sam was lying on the ground. His whole body was heaving as he panted and coughed, trying to get his breath.

CHAPTER FIVE

"**A**ll right, Sam." Mike Turner spoke in a soothing voice as he gently put his stethoscope against the collie's heart. "Good boy."

"Is he —" Neil swallowed hard, not able to finish the sentence, staring at his dog stretched out on the sofa. Uncle Jack, who was watching anxiously with Emily and Sarah, put a comforting arm around his shoulders.

Mike Turner made a thorough examination of Sam's abdomen before straightening up to look at Neil.

"It's OK, Neil. Sam's going to make it this time. This was just a scare."

Neil felt his legs buckle with relief. He sat down with a thump on a nearby chair.

"But it does go to show that he's got to be kept quiet and avoid getting overexcited," Mike continued. "Getting frightened or excited raises Sam's heart rate, and then, because his heart's weak, it can't cope."

"I know," Neil muttered, feeling guilty, although it wasn't his fault. The minutes that had ticked away while they waited for Mike Turner to arrive had been the worst of his whole life.

"I think I'd better keep Sam at the clinic for a few days," Mike said, "just to keep an eye on him. I'm pretty certain he'll be OK, but I'd like to be sure."

Neil nodded, reaching out to pet Sam's head. The collie pushed his muzzle into Neil's hand, acting a little more like his old self.

"I'll take him with me now," Mike said as he put his stethoscope away. "Get his leash, will you, Neil? He should be able to walk to the car."

Mike gently urged Sam to his feet and led him very slowly down the hall. Neil and the others followed. Just as Mike opened the front door, Hasheem and Chris raced up the driveway, looking very excited. Both of them were carrying several newspapers, which they waved at Neil and the others.

"Hey, Neil! You and Molly are all over the papers!" Chris yelled.

"Sorry we're late. We both overslept!" Hasheem added. Then he stopped when he saw Neil's face.

"Sam collapsed," Neil explained quietly. "But Mike thinks he's going to be OK this time."

"What happened?" Hasheem asked anxiously as Mike made Sam comfortable in the back of his car.

Neil told them about the All Spice fans and the way they'd tried to get to Molly.

"What a bunch of idiots!" Chris said angrily.

Neil leaned into Mike's car and rubbed his head against Sam's.

"Bye, Sam," he whispered.

"I'll keep you posted, Neil," Mike Turner said as he started the engine. "And drop in to see Sam whenever you like."

Neil nodded. He stood and watched as Mike's car pulled onto the main road and set off in the direction of Compton.

"Hey, listen to the dogs back there!" Hasheem said as the sound of barking intensified. "What's going on?"

"We haven't fed or walked them yet!" Emily explained. "And it's after ten o'clock!"

"Well, we'd better get going. Right?" Chris said briskly.

Neil was the last to go back into the house. He felt tired and drained, as if he had all the problems of the world on his shoulders — well, all the problems of King Street Kennels, anyway. Now he had Sam to worry about, too. And it was still five days before his parents would be home. They hadn't called again, either, which meant that they still hadn't come to a decision about the fate of the kennel.

Neil sighed. Why had he ever thought they could

run the kennel on their own? So far he felt as if he'd made a complete mess of things. He didn't even care that his picture was in the papers. If he hadn't let Kerry Kirby's dog come to stay at King Street, none of this would have happened. The press wouldn't have turned up, neither would the fans, and Sam would still be all right. He'd been right when he'd said that they'd taken on a whole lot of trouble by boarding Molly at King Street Kennels.

Just when Neil thought he couldn't get any more depressed, things started to improve. For one thing, Uncle Jack decided that he would try to manage without his painkillers, and he helped out with the walking and feeding that morning.

"My arm's still a bit sore, but I think I can put up with it," he said cheerfully, spooning dog food into dishes with his good arm. "Anyway, I don't think I was much use when I was popping those pills!" He glanced at Neil, who was opening a bag of dog biscuits. "You should have told me, Neil."

"Oh, we managed all right," Neil assured him, but Uncle Jack grimaced.

"Your mom and dad would have forty fits if they knew you kids had been doing everything around here for the last few days!"

"Well, I won't tell them if you won't!" Neil managed a smile. He was feeling much better now that Uncle Jack was back to his old self. Grown-ups could be a pain at times, but they did have their uses! And even a one-handed Uncle Jack was a help while they were so busy.

Neil cheered up even more when Mike called just after lunch to say that Sam was improving.

"His heart rate's back to normal, and he's just had a small meal," Mike told him. "He's doing fine."

"Thanks, Mike," Neil said gratefully. "I'll come over to see him later this afternoon."

Now that he was assured of Sam's recovery, Neil could relax a little. But he knew very well that a time would definitely come when Sam would get sick and would not get better. That was the hardest thing of all to bear.

To take his mind off Sam, Neil decided to give Jake another training session that afternoon and let Molly join in, too. Whatever had happened, he was glad that Molly had come to King Street. He wouldn't have missed getting to know her for anything. She was one of the most lovable doggy personalities he'd ever come across.

"So you think you can train her?" Chris asked doubtfully as Neil led Molly into Red's Barn. Molly was doing her favorite trick of hanging on to the leash with her teeth and trying to wrench it out of Neil's hand, and even Neil had to admit she didn't look particularly trainable. Chris was holding Jake in his arms, and as soon as Molly saw the puppy, she dragged Neil across the barn toward him.

"Hasheem had to go," Chris said. "But he promised to be back tonight."

"Good," Neil said gratefully. He could hardly believe how all their friends had rallied around to give them a hand. He didn't know how he would ever repay them, giving up their vacation like this.

"Here, hold Molly for me, will you?" Neil made sure he had Jake's attention, then he raised his hand. The puppy immediately plumped down on his bottom and looked expectantly at Neil. "Good boy, Jake!"

"He's very obedient. He obviously takes after his dad!" Chris said admiringly.

"Well, he's had the best training available since he was tiny." Neil laughed. "But he *is* a fast learner."

Molly, for once, was sitting perfectly still, ears pricked and eyes alert, watching what was going on.

"Now it's your turn, Molly." Neil positioned the dog in front of him and took a dog treat from his pocket. Molly's attention was immediately riveted on Neil's hand. As Neil raised it, Molly sat down on her haunches, her bottom going down as her head moved upward.

"Good girl!" Neil said as Molly wolfed down the treat. He took another one out of his pocket, and this time Molly sat down as soon as he raised his hand. Neil blinked in amazement.

"Wow!" Chris said, impressed. "She's got it already!"

Neil tried again several times, in case it had been a fluke. But it wasn't. Molly was proving to be an exceptionally intelligent dog.

"She might have had some basic training before she went to the shelter, I suppose," Neil said, thrilled at the way Molly had responded to him. "I might be able to teach her a lot before Kerry Kirby comes back for her next week!"

So the day had ended a lot better than it had started, Neil thought drowsily as he snuggled down under his blanket. Sam had been looking more lively when

Neil had visited him, and Mike had said that he could come home in a day or two. Uncle Jack was back to normal now that he wasn't taking those painkillers, and Molly, contrary to all expectations, was proving to be a delight to train. Also, Kate would be in bright and early tomorrow morning. Neil smiled to himself as his eyes began to close. Maybe he hadn't done such a bad job of running the kennel after all. . . .

"Neil! Neil, wake up!"

Sarah's voice rang in Neil's ears as he lay fast asleep in his warm bed. He struggled to open his eyes and dragged himself upright. Sarah was standing next to his bed, her eyes wide with fear.

"What — what's up, Squirt?" Neil mumbled, rubbing his eyes. It didn't feel as if he'd been asleep for very long, but the dial on his alarm clock read 2:20 A.M. "Can't you sleep?"

"There are two people in the backyard!" Sarah whispered fearfully. "And they're trying to get into the kennel!"

CHAPTER SIX

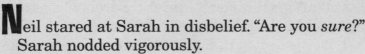

Neil stared at Sarah in disbelief. "Are you *sure*?"

Sarah nodded vigorously.

"Fudge was running around in his wheel, and he woke me up," she explained. "I got up to go to the bathroom, and I saw them!"

Neil climbed out of bed and went over to the window. There was a security light in the corner of the courtyard, but he couldn't see anyone. Then he stiffened. Two shadows were moving around outside Kennel Block One.

He turned urgently to Sarah. "Why didn't you get Uncle Jack?"

Sarah pouted. "I tried to, but he wouldn't wake up!"

Neil's heart sank. His uncle must have taken one of his pills before going to sleep. Despite Uncle Jack's brave attempts to do without the painkillers, he had looked exhausted and pale by the end of the day.

"Sarah, go and wake him up," he said, groping for his sneakers. "Pour a glass of cold water over him if you have to, but do it somehow!"

Sarah nodded and hurried out.

"What's going on?" Emily stumbled into Neil's room, rubbing her eyes.

"Intruders," Neil said briefly, pulling a sweater on over his pajamas.

"What, you mean burglars?" Emily gasped.

"They're trying to get into Kennel Block One." Neil led Emily to the window and pointed across the courtyard. The shadowy figures could just be seen, hovering around the door of the kennel block.

"But what *for*?" Emily asked, puzzled.

"I don't know," Neil began. Then he stopped, the color draining from his face. "Maybe they're after Molly! I think we forgot to switch the alarm system on."

"Molly!" Emily repeated, horrified. "You don't think they're trying to kidnap her?"

"They might be," Neil said grimly as he brushed past his sister and hurried downstairs. "Kerry's rich, isn't she? She could afford to pay a big ransom. You'd better call the police, Em. I'm going to try to stop them."

"Neil, you can't!" Emily dashed after him. "Let's get Uncle Jack."

"Sarah's trying to wake him now." Neil put his

jacket on and slipped a flashlight into the pocket. "I
think he must've had one of his painkillers, because
he's fast asleep."

"Well, I'm coming with you, then!" Emily said in a
determined voice, grabbing her coat.

"Somebody's got to call the police —" Neil began,
but Emily was already opening the front door.

"If we wait any longer, it might be too late!"

Neil gave up arguing and followed his sister out
into the cool night air. Emily was right — they couldn't
wait for the police in case the intruders got away with
Molly, assuming that Kerry Kirby's dog *was* their
target.

"What should we do?" Emily asked Neil in a quiet
voice.

"Try to frighten them off," Neil answered, hoping
he wasn't going to be confronted by two big, burly
dognappers. He switched on his flashlight and
scanned the beam across the courtyard to Kennel
Block One. "Who's there?" he shouted bravely.

The two figures outside the kennel block froze in
the sudden blaze of light. Neil's and Emily's mouths
fell open in amazement as they saw two teenage
girls wearing All Spice T-shirts, cameras around
their necks, staring back at them sheepishly.

"We just wanted to get some pictures of ourselves
with Kerry's dog," one of the girls muttered as Uncle
Jack glared at them. "We didn't mean any harm."

"Didn't mean any harm?" Neil exploded. "You almost scared us all to death!"

Luckily Sarah had managed to shake their uncle awake, and he had hurried out into the courtyard just as Neil and Emily were confronting the two girls. He had brought them into the kitchen to find out exactly what was going on.

"All right, Neil, I'll handle this," Jack said, staring grimly at the two girls. "You've behaved very irresponsibly. You know that, don't you?"

Both the girls looked totally embarrassed and nodded.

"And I suppose your parents don't know where you are, either?" Uncle Jack raised his eyebrows at them.

"They think we're staying at each other's houses," the girls mumbled together.

"Well, I think you'd better give me your names and

phone numbers," Uncle Jack said sternly. One of the girls was named Lucy Jackson, the other was Natalie Webb, and they both lived in Compton.

"How did you get in?" Emily asked.

"We rode our bikes over from Compton," Natalie explained sheepishly. "Then we climbed over the gate in the field at the back."

"You're lucky we didn't call the police!" Neil pointed out. Although the girls were just harmless All Spice fans, he was still upset. They'd given everyone a real scare. And it made him think about whether Molly was really safe at King Street.

The two girls turned pale, and Neil couldn't help feeling a bit sorry for them. He glanced at Emily, who looked as if she felt the same. "Uncle Jack, can I talk to you for a minute?" Neil said as his uncle headed off toward the phone.

Uncle Jack stopped. "What is it, Neil?"

"I was thinking, maybe we could let those girls meet Molly," Neil said in a low voice. "Just for a few minutes."

Uncle Jack looked surprised. "I'm not sure that's a good idea, Neil. After all, they've caused a lot of trouble."

"I know," Neil admitted. "But their parents are going to be really angry, so I can't help feeling sorry for them."

Uncle Jack smiled. "I know what you mean. I

wouldn't want to be in their shoes when their parents get here, either! All right. Go get Molly."

Neil went over to Natalie and Lucy. "My uncle Jack is calling your parents," he said, and the girls' faces fell even farther. "While you're waiting for them to get here, do you want to meet Molly?"

Lucy and Natalie couldn't believe their ears.

"You mean it?" Lucy said breathlessly. "We can *see* Molly?"

Neil nodded. "Just for a minute or two."

"Thank you!" Natalie stammered, looking as if someone had just told her she'd won a million pounds.

"Good idea, Neil!" said Emily approvingly, giving him a thumbs-up.

Neil grabbed the keys to Kennel Block One and went outside. All the dogs were asleep in their baskets, but they stirred when they sensed his presence, and some of them started barking. Molly was already standing by the door of her pen, poking her muzzle through the wire mesh. She was delighted to see Neil so early in the morning and leaped up at him, barking.

"Come on, Molly," Neil said, clipping the leash to her collar. "Time to go and meet some of your fans!"

As Neil led Molly into the kitchen, the two girls looked as excited as if Kerry Kirby herself had just walked in. They stared at Molly, their faces full of awe.

"Can we pet her?" Natalie asked eagerly.

"Of course," Neil replied. Molly was beside herself with joy at seeing Jake again, as well as so many people crowded into the kitchen, and she was rushing from one person to the other and pawing at their legs. She sniffed Natalie and Lucy with interest, then launched herself at them, barking a welcome.

"Oh, she's gorgeous!" said Lucy, kneeling down so that she could give Molly a hug.

"I think that's enough," Jack said when they heard a couple of cars pulling onto the drive. "It sounds like your parents are here to get you!"

Lucy's parents and Natalie's parents came in together, full of apologies for their daughters' behavior and threatening to ground them for life. Neil was glad that he'd let the two girls see Molly — they were obviously going to be in big trouble for sneaking out without their parents' knowledge!

"Well, I think that's enough excitement for one night!" Uncle Jack said as he closed the door behind them. "And tomorrow I'm going to see Doc Harvey to ask him to prescribe some weaker painkillers for me." He glanced at Neil and Emily. "I would never have forgiven myself if anything had happened to you two tonight. It was my own fault for not checking the alarms. You should have called the police and not gone out there on your own."

"We thought someone might be trying to kidnap Molly," Neil explained.

Uncle Jack turned pale. "Heavens! You mean — to get ransom money out of Kerry Kirby? I never thought of that!" He frowned. "I'm beginning to wish we hadn't taken Molly in. She's been nothing but trouble so far!"

"It's not Molly's fault," Neil put in quickly. "But I think we should be extra careful from now on."

Uncle Jack nodded. "Well, I'll take Molly back to her pen now, and I'll double-check that everything's locked up safely."

Neil frowned. He still wasn't happy. What had happened tonight made him realize that Molly might need extra protection. "Uncle Jack," he said slowly. "I think we should move Molly into the house with us."

Uncle Jack raised his eyebrows. "I thought your parents had a strict rule about that."

"This is a special case, though," Neil argued. "We have to be sure that Molly is safe."

"It would be awful if anything happened to her," Emily chimed in. "And it would be really bad publicity for the kennel, too."

"Yes, maybe you're right," Uncle Jack said slowly. "Do you think she'll be comfortable in here, though?"

"She'll be fine as long as she's with Jake." Neil let Molly off the leash, and she immediately dived under the table where Jake, who was tired out after all the excitement, had curled up for a snooze. Molly nudged the puppy gently, and Jake opened a sleepy

eye, then snuggled up against the older dog. "See?"
Neil knelt down and patted both dogs on the head.
He was sure that this was the best solution for
everyone, especially for Molly. "Good night, you two.
See you in the morning."

CHAPTER SEVEN

"**M**olly!" Neil looked around the kitchen, aghast. "Molly, what have you *done*?"

It was the following morning. After the excitement of the previous night, Neil had slept in. Again. So had everyone else, except for Molly and Jake, who were very much awake. Molly rushed over to greet Neil. Jake emerged from under the remains of the tablecloth, which had been dragged off the table and ripped to shreds. The rug had been chewed, and somehow the two dogs had gotten hold of a roll of paper towels and torn it apart. The room looked as if it had been hit by a snowstorm.

Just at that moment Emily came in, yawning. She stopped dead when she saw the mess. "Oh, *Molly!*"

"I think we'd better get it cleaned up fast, before Uncle Jack sees it!" Neil threw the ruined tablecloth into the garbage can. "Or he might change his mind about keeping Molly in the house!"

A knock on the back door made them both look up. Kate McGuire was standing there, smiling at them.

"Kate!" Neil hurried across to unlock the door, and Kate came in, looking relaxed and tan, her long blond hair tied back in a ponytail.

"What's the matter with all you sleepyheads?" she asked teasingly. "It's a good thing that I've got my own keys to get in — I started work an hour ago!"

"Did you have a good vacation?" Emily asked her.

"Fantastic, thanks." Kate glanced around the kitchen. "But it looks as if you've been having even more excitement here! Oh, hello. Who's this?" Seeing someone new in the room, Molly had rushed over to investigate and was jumping up at Kate to get her attention. "Don't tell me — I think I know! I've heard all about you and a certain pop star! But what's Molly doing in the house?"

Neil explained briefly about the two intruders, and Kate frowned.

"I don't suppose your parents were too happy about that!"

Neil glanced at Emily. "Mom and Dad aren't here, Kate. A lot's been happening since you were last at King Street."

While the three of them cleared up the kitchen, Neil told Kate about Great-aunt Victoria's will, their parents' vacation, Uncle Jack's injury, and Sam's trip to the vet. He didn't mention the fact that their parents were thinking of selling the kennel — after all, Kate's job was at stake, and he didn't want to worry her. But Kate was too sharp not to see the implications.

"If Bob and Carole have gone away at one of the busiest times of the year, they must be thinking about making some major changes to their lifestyle." One look at Neil and Emily told Kate she'd hit the nail on the head. "Are they seriously thinking about leaving the kennel?"

Neil nodded miserably. "It's an option. They haven't made up their minds yet."

Kate looked upset. "Well, maybe I'm being selfish, but I love working here. I hope they decide to stay."

"So do we," Emily and Neil said together. They heard footsteps overhead. Neil added urgently, "Sarah doesn't know yet, so don't say anything to her."

"I won't," Kate promised. "And, Neil — I'm really glad Sam's going to be OK. This place wouldn't be the same without him."

Neil felt as if a huge burden had been lifted from his shoulders now that Kate was back. She was efficient and capable with the dogs, and even though Neil and Emily still had to help out, they didn't have to run around as much as they'd done before. It was lucky that Kate was back today, Neil thought. Hasheem's parents were taking him to see his grandmother, so he wouldn't be able to come to the kennel at all, and Chris had called to say he'd be by later that morning; he had a dentist appointment to go to first. With Kate around, Neil wouldn't need to rely on his friends so much.

"You look tired, Neil." Kate eyed him critically as they went into Kennel Block One. "Why don't you take a break? I can manage."

Neil hesitated. He *did* feel exhausted. The events of the last few days had knocked him out.

"I don't want to leave you on your own," he began, but Kate grinned at him.

"Go on. I've already sent Emily packing! If you two don't rest, you'll be tired out by the time you go back to school! Your uncle and I can manage."

Neil felt a sudden urge to get out into the countryside and take Jake for a good long walk to relax. "All right," he agreed. "I think I'll take Jake up to the ridge."

"Why don't you take Molly, too?" Kate suggested. "She looks like she should let off some steam!"

Neil frowned. He had been reluctant to take Molly out of the kennel again, but Kate was right. The dog needed to release some of her pent-up energy — and they'd survived the press, the fans, and the intruders so far. What else could possibly go wrong?

"All right," he said. "But Kate, could you check on Daisy, the little poodle? She hasn't settled in very well. I think she misses her owner."

"Will do," Kate agreed.

"Oh, and Robbie's had an eye infection. Mike left some drops for him, so could you — ?"

"Neil, relax!" Kate told him with a grin. "I'll handle it all. Now will you *please* go?"

Twenty minutes later Neil headed up the path that led to the ridge, Jake and Molly bounding along at his side. He realized that he was enjoying himself for the first time in days. The sun was shining and the air was crisp and fresh. Neil wondered what the weather was like in Scotland, where his parents were. He hoped it was good and that they were making the most of their trip to clear their heads and discuss the future. Neil pushed the thought aside. He didn't want to spoil the beautiful morning. Whatever happened, he'd just have to learn to deal with it.

He let Jake off his leash, and the puppy raced off happily, then came back to see if Molly was joining him. Molly stared up at Neil pleadingly with her big brown eyes and barked.

Neil hesitated. He couldn't see any harm in letting Molly run free, too. After all, she probably wouldn't stray off anywhere while Jake was around, and she needed the exercise. He knelt down and unclipped the leash. "Off you go, Molly!"

Molly raced after Jake, quivering all over with joy, and the two dogs began to chase each other along the ridge. Neil laughed and walked slowly after them. He would have time to give Molly and Jake a longer training session today now that Kate was back. He was definitely going to suggest to Kerry Kirby that she get another dog to keep Molly company, whatever Emily said. He was sure Kerry would agree, once she saw Jake and Molly together.

A loud bark interrupted Neil's thoughts. He looked up and his heart sank when he saw a rabbit racing along the ridge, with Molly in hot pursuit, ears back, her shaggy body trembling with eagerness. Jake, too, was running along behind her as fast as his short little legs could carry him.

Neil let out a groan and set off after them. "Molly,

come back!" he shouted, knowing full well that she wouldn't.

True to form, Molly ignored him. All her attention was fixed on the fascinating furry brown creature that was running in front of her, and she wasn't going to stop until she caught up with it.

"Molly!" Neil called again, panting as he chased after them. "Molly, come here!" He shouldn't have let her off the leash, Neil told himself, feeling guilty, but at least it was fairly safe up here on the ridge. It wasn't as if they were near any busy roads. They were surrounded by fields and countryside, so neither of the dogs was in any real danger. As long as Neil kept them in sight, he would be able to catch up with them when the rabbit disappeared down a hole. If only the rabbit would hurry up and do that, Neil thought as he gasped for breath. He wasn't sure he could run at this pace much longer.

As if the rabbit were reading Neil's mind, it suddenly swerved sideways and disappeared down one of the many narrow holes in the surface of the ridge. The ground beneath contained a labyrinth of caves and tunnels and was a favorite area with spelunkers, although most of the holes on the surface were too small for anyone to enter.

At last! Neil thought triumphantly when he saw Molly and Jake skid to a halt by the hole and start barking. "Molly!" he yelled with what little breath he had left. "Jake!"

Jake obediently started trotting back toward Neil, but Molly was sniffing around the hole and barking with all her might. Then, to Neil's horror, he saw the dog stick her head down the hole and start to wriggle her body through, too, in an attempt to follow the rabbit.

"Molly!" Neil shouted, turning white with fear. *"Molly!* Stay there, girl! Don't move!" If Molly went underground and got lost in the tunnels, she might never be seen again. Neil forced himself to run faster, although his lungs were almost bursting. He had to reach Molly before she went through the hole. *He had to.*

Molly was halfway into the hole when Neil raced desperately up the ridge toward her. She wasn't in-

terested in Neil but was staring down into the hole, as if she was trying to find the rabbit.

"Good girl, Molly!" Neil panted as he rushed up to her. "Now just stay there."

But then, just as Neil got to her, Molly lunged forward and disappeared. Frantically, Neil launched himself forward, trying to catch hold of her shaggy tail, but it whisked tantalizingly out of his reach before he could grab it. He was too late.

Molly had vanished.

CHAPTER EIGHT

"Molly!" Neil yelled at the top of his voice, bending over the hole. He couldn't see a thing because it was pitch-black down there. He couldn't even see how deep the hole was, and he hoped that Molly hadn't hurt herself scrambling through it. "Molly, come back!"

Jake whined and pawed at the ground around the hole, sensing something was wrong. Neil clipped the puppy's leash on quickly, just in case he decided to follow Molly.

"Molly!" Neil shouted again. "Where are you?"

Then Neil heard a ghostly bark coming from underground. He leaned in as far as he could, his nerves stretched to the breaking point. Then the barking died away, and there was silence.

"Molly!"

This time there was no answer. Neil felt dizzy with fear as he imagined Molly heading deeper and deeper into the labyrinthine cave system and never being heard from again. There was only one thing he could do. He'd have to follow her. But what about Jake? He didn't want to take the puppy into what might be a dangerous situation.

Neil hesitated, then made a quick decision. He reached out and looped the end of Jake's leash over a jagged piece of rock. He wasn't sure if it would keep Jake there for long, but it was the best he could do, and he and Molly might be back soon anyway.

Suddenly, with a surge of hope, Neil remembered that he still had a flashlight in his jacket pocket from when he'd gone to check on the intruders the night before. Quickly he pulled it out and switched it on, pointing the beam down into the hole. To his relief, he saw that it wasn't very far down to the floor of the cave.

Neil patted Jake on the head reassuringly and then slid into the hole, feetfirst. It was a tight squeeze, but he took off his jacket and managed it. He scrabbled against the rock face below him, feeling for a foothold.

"I'll be back as soon as I can, Jake," he promised, and climbed down.

Jake barked in confusion. His master had gone.

*　　*　　*

Neil made his way cautiously down the side of the hole. The flashlight wasn't much help to him because he needed both hands to grip the rock face, so he slipped it into his pocket. But as soon as his feet touched the ground, he switched the light on again, with a sigh of relief. The air was damp, and he could feel a wetness lapping around his ankles. It would have been really scary if he hadn't had the flashlight with him.

Right away Neil saw that there was only one way Molly could have gone, and that was down a small tunnel on his right. Too worried about the dog to let his own fears get the better of him, he began to crawl after her on his hands and knees, trying to aim the light ahead of him at the same time. The tunnel sloped downward, making Neil feel as if he were crawling right into the center of the earth, and the roof was so low in places that he had to lie on his stomach and wriggle his way through.

Neil came out into a much bigger cave, one he could just about stand up in. Quickly he moved the light around, noting that there were three tunnels of different sizes leading off it. His heart sank. How would he know which way Molly had gone?

"Molly!" he yelled, his voice echoing in the cave. "Molly!"

Then Neil heard it — a bark that seemed to be coming from the tunnel closest to him. Hoping he hadn't been deceived by an echo, Neil headed toward it, praying that he would find Molly before she went any deeper underground.

"What's the matter with you?" Emily said to Chris as he stumbled into the kennel office, clutching the side of his face. "You look as if you've had ten teeth pulled!"

"I *feel* like I've had ten teeth pulled!" Chris complained. "I've had two fillings, and my mouth's still half numb! Where's Neil?"

Before Emily could reply, the phone rang. Emily answered it and her eyes lit up. "Dad! You haven't called for ages!"

"Sorry, sweetheart," said Bob. "We've had a lot to talk about. How're things? How're Neil and Sarah?"

"We're all fine," Emily said quickly. "Have you — have you decided anything yet?"

"We're getting there," Bob said. Emily noted that her father did sound a lot more cheerful. "Going away like this was just what we needed."

"You *will* be home on Tuesday, won't you?" Emily demanded anxiously.

"Of course we will!" Bob assured her. "Now, is Jack around? I'd like to talk with him for a minute."

Just at that moment Uncle Jack turned up at the office door to see who was calling, and Emily handed the phone to him.

"Hello, Bob!" Jack said cheerfully. "Yes, everything's fine."

"Where's Neil?" Chris asked Emily in a hushed voice.

"He took Jake and Molly up to the ridge for a walk," Emily said. "Kate's back, so she told us both to go and relax. She said we've been working too hard!"

"Neil won't be relaxing much if he's walking that energetic dog!" Chris chuckled. Then he stopped laughing suddenly and squinted up the driveway. "Hey, Em, did you say Neil took Jake with him?"

"Yes, why?" Emily said, then her eyes widened.

Jake was scurrying up the driveway toward the office, yapping anxiously, his leash trailing along behind him. Emily ran over to the door, and Jake made a beeline for her, leaping into her arms as if he was really glad to see a friendly face.

"What's he doing here?" Chris asked with a frown.

"And where's Neil?" Emily added, looking worried.

"Maybe Jake just got away from him!" Chris smiled. "We'll probably see him come charging after him in a minute, with Molly right behind!"

Emily grinned. "You're probably right. Those two animals are quite a handful!" She and Chris waited in the office doorway for a moment or two, expecting to see Neil and Molly any second. But neither of them appeared.

"I don't like this." Emily stared anxiously at Chris.

"Neil would never let Jake run away from him like this unless —"

"Unless something was wrong." Chris finished the sentence for her. "Why don't we go up to the ridge and see if we can find him?"

"Uncle Jack!" Emily said urgently as he said his good-byes to Bob and put the phone down. "Jake came back without Neil and Molly. We think something might be wrong!"

Uncle Jack frowned. "And there I am, telling your dad that we're all fine! I'm sure Neil's all right, but maybe we'd better go take a look. We'll leave Sarah with Kate."

"We'll take Jake with us, too," Emily said, hugging the puppy to her chest. "He might be able to lead us to Neil and Molly."

Neil was wet, cold, and tired. And he was beginning to panic. For the past hour, he had been through so many caves and so many tunnels he had completely lost his way, and he still hadn't found Molly. All the walls looked the same. Every so often he thought he heard a bark, and he kept going in that direction, but by now he was wondering if he was imagining things. There was simply no sign of Molly anywhere.

Then, suddenly, he heard a loud bark. Neil crawled down the tunnel as fast as he could and came out into a really high and spacious cave. To his relief,

Molly was sitting on a rocky ledge, wagging her tail and giving little barks of joy.

"Molly!" Neil rushed over, picked the dog up, and buried his face in her damp fur. She was as wet and dirty as he was, but he didn't care. He'd found her, and she was safe!

"Come on, girl," Neil murmured, shaking all over with relief. "Let's go back." He just hoped he would be able to remember his way. Some of the caves he'd passed through had had lots of tunnels leading in and out of them. He wasn't sure he could find the way back, but he had to try.

Molly, however, had other ideas. She wriggled out of Neil's arms and headed over to another tunnel.

"No, Molly!" Neil said, alarmed. "That'll just take us deeper underground! *This* way!" And he pointed to the tunnel he'd just crawled out of.

Molly wouldn't move. She started barking. Neil grabbed her and took her back across the cave, but Molly refused to go down the tunnel that he wanted her to. Neil couldn't carry her because he had to get down on his hands and knees. Short of pushing the little dog down the opening ahead of him, he didn't know what he could do. As soon as he put Molly down, though, she headed straight back over to the other tunnel.

Neil hesitated. Molly seemed to know where she was going, and he wasn't sure he could find his way back anyway, so what did he have to lose?

"All right," he told Molly. "You win! I'll follow you."

Molly wagged her tail, then turned and plunged down the tunnel. Neil went after her. The way ahead was narrow, barely big enough for Neil to squeeze through in some places. Although Molly was leading the way, she never went very far without stopping and turning around to check that Neil was still there.

"Here I am, Molly!" Neil assured her as, weary and wet, he struggled along on his hands and knees. "Keep going, girl!"

Molly seemed to understand what Neil was saying and continued to sniff her way down the tunnel. Neil dragged himself after her, hoping desperately that he was doing the right thing. He was putting his faith in Molly to lead them both to safety, and he hoped she wouldn't let him down.

Suddenly, Neil noticed the beam of his flashlight beginning to flicker, and his heart plummeted. He stopped and gave the flashlight a shake, hoping that it had just gotten damp, but he could tell that the battery was running out fast. It certainly wouldn't last much longer. Neil swallowed hard at the thought of being plunged into darkness, far underground, unable to see where he was going.

Now more than ever, Molly was his only hope.

CHAPTER NINE

"**T**here's no sign of them!" Emily looked around the ridge anxiously. "Where can they be?"

"Maybe they never came up here," Chris suggested, but Emily shook her head.

"No, Neil told Kate he was coming up here." She looked at her uncle with wide, scared eyes. "You don't think — you don't think they've been *kidnapped*, do you, Uncle Jack?"

"I'm sure they haven't," Uncle Jack said reassuringly, but he couldn't help sounding worried.

"What's the matter with Jake?" Chris asked when he noticed the puppy pawing wildly at the ground next to a narrow hole. "Come on, Jake! You're supposed to be helping us find Neil and Molly!"

Emily's eyes lit up. "Maybe he is! Maybe this is the last place he saw them!"

"But where would they have gone?" Chris asked, with a frown.

They all looked around, but there was still no sign of the missing pair. Then Emily looked down at the hole and gasped.

"Look!" cried Emily. "It's Neil's jacket! Uncle Jack!" she said, her eyes wide. "Do you think Neil and Molly could be down *there*?" And she pointed at the hole.

"What on earth would they be doing down there?" Uncle Jack asked, puzzled. "Neil wouldn't do that — he knows how dangerous it is!"

"Maybe he didn't have any choice," Emily suggested. "Not if Molly went down there first!"

"You mean that crazy Molly went down this hole, and Neil went after her?" Uncle Jack asked.

The discarded jacket lay scrunched up beside the hole. Uncle Jack knelt down and picked it up. His face clouded over. Handing the jacket to Emily, Jack examined the ground by the hole more closely. "There's definitely been something going on here," he said grimly. "The grass is all flattened, and look at these footprints."

"They look like they were made by a pair of sneakers," Chris said, also squatting down to take a look.

"Neil was wearing sneakers this morning!" Emily pointed out in a shaky voice.

"But even if Neil went after Molly, he wouldn't leave Jake to go home on his own, would he?" Chris asked.

"Maybe he thought he'd tied him up safely, but Jake managed to get away," Emily suggested.

"That must be it." Uncle Jack stood up, looking somber. "We'd better go back and call Sergeant Moorhead to organize a search. If they're lost in those caves . . ." He didn't finish the sentence, but Emily and Chris knew what he had been going to say. If Neil and Molly were lost underground, they might never see them again.

The battery had now died completely, and Neil was crawling through the pitch-black tunnel. He was very scared, but Molly seemed to know how he was feeling and had slowed her pace so that she was just in front of him all the time. If Neil reached out, he could touch her damp fur, which he found very reassuring.

"Good girl, Molly," he whispered, stretching his hand into the darkness to pet her. "You're doing fine."

Molly licked Neil's hand and continued slowly down the tunnel. She still seemed full of energy, but Neil was so tired he could hardly move. Every bone in his body was aching, and his hands and knees were sore from crawling along the rocky floor. He was sure that he had made the right decision to follow Molly, but still he couldn't help feeling scared, as well as worried about Jake. What if they couldn't find a way out?

"Where did all these reporters come from?" Emily gasped as she looked around the ridge. There were ten photographers and as many reporters, kept at bay about fifty yards away by a couple of policemen. Jake Fielding of the *Compton News* was one of them.

"News travels fast," Sergeant Moorhead replied. He was a middle-aged gray-haired man who knew Bob Parker well. "Especially when a pop star's dog is involved."

"Where's that rescue team?" Uncle Jack demanded, looking pale with anxiety. "It's been nearly an hour since we called them."

Everyone was desperate with worry, and it showed on their faces. They stood around the hole, hoping Neil's head might miraculously pop out of it and surprise them all.

"Here they come now," Sergeant Moorhead said quickly. A team of five men dressed in warm, waterproof clothes was hurrying toward them, carrying coils of rope over their shoulders.

Emily clenched her fists. "They've got to find Neil and Molly," she muttered. "Anything could have happened to them."

"They will," Chris assured her, wishing he felt as confident as he sounded.

"We think they went down this way," Sergeant Moorhead said to Colin Grahame, the leader of the rescue team, pointing at the hole. "We tried shouting but haven't heard any reply."

Colin, a big, burly man with red hair, frowned. "That's too small for us to get through. We'll have to go in another way, but as near to this as we can."

Emily bit her lip. Everything was taking so long.

The tunnel began to widen out into a small cave. Molly barked loudly as Neil got to his feet, thankfully. As he did so, it suddenly struck him that he could *see* — the cave wasn't as dark as the tunnel they'd just crawled out of. It was then that Neil glanced up and noticed a small patch of daylight overhead in the roof of the cave. He stared at it, dazed, for a few seconds, blinking in the sunshine that slanted through the hole, hardly able to believe his eyes. Molly had led him to safety! Neil gasped with relief. He had been right to put his trust in her.

"Good girl, Molly!" he said, rumpling her damp, furry coat. "Good girl!"

They still had one problem, though.

Neil couldn't see how he and Molly were going to get up to the hole and back outside. Although it wasn't very high, the rock face looked smooth, with few footholds, and it was also very steep. Neil wasn't sure that he could climb up there, especially as he would have to carry Molly, too. He and Molly would have to make a noise and maybe attract someone's attention, but that could take hours.

He began to think that he would never get out.

Molly was barking and scrabbling about frantically at the foot of the rock face. Neil's eyes were slowly adjusting to the daylight, and when he looked over at Molly, he saw a shape running up the wall. He squinted slightly and could now see clearly a very narrow wire ladder resting against the rock face. It looked like it led right up to the hole in the roof.

"You're a genius, Molly!" Neil knelt down and gave the dog a hug. "I *knew* you'd get us out!"

Neil could climb up the ladder, but Molly couldn't, so he would have to carry her. The only alternative was to leave Molly behind and go for help, but Neil knew that if he did, Molly might wander off back into the cave system and be lost forever. Quickly he made a decision.

"Come on, Molly." He picked the dog up and placed her inside his warm baggy sweater, tucking it into his jeans so she wouldn't fall out. Her face peered up at him from the stretched V-neck, and he gently petted her forehead. "We're going up that ladder, so please, Molly, keep as still as you can."

The ladder felt incredibly flimsy as Neil climbed higher, his every movement slow and deliberate. It swayed gently each time he placed his foot on one of the thin rungs, sending his stomach churning every few seconds. He didn't dare look down. The ceiling of the cave was higher than he'd thought, and the small patch of daylight above him didn't seem to be getting much closer, even though he felt as if he'd been climbing for ages.

So far, Molly had been as good as gold. She was keeping perfectly still, but Neil could feel her heart beating quickly against his chest. He could sense that she was as nervous as he was, but if they could both keep cool, they could make it to safety. Molly had done all the hard work so far — now it was his turn.

The patch of daylight came nearer and nearer, the strong light making Neil's eyes water after being underground for so long. Molly raised her head slightly and sniffed the fresh air streaming through the hole. Then she started to bark happily.

"Yeah, we're nearly there!" Neil told her triumphantly. "Just a little farther!"

"What's that noise?" Emily said suddenly.

"What noise?" Uncle Jack and Chris said together.

"I thought I heard a dog barking!" Emily gasped, standing as still as a statue and listening hard. Everyone else who was standing around listened, too.

"You must be imagining things," Uncle Jack said.

Colin Grahame raised his hand. "Shh! I think I heard something, too!"

Everyone fell silent then, even the reporters and the photographers. For a few seconds, no one could hear anything. Then, suddenly, there was the sound of a bark, echoing across the ridge. This time everyone heard it.

"It's Molly! I know it is!" Emily shouted. "It's coming from over there!"

She pointed a little way up the ridge.

And ran.

Neil and Molly had to squeeze through the hole together, but it was narrow, and maneuvering with Molly tucked inside his sweater was difficult. For one horrible moment Neil thought he was going to get stuck, but then, with a final wriggle, he was through. As he crawled out into the daylight, Neil almost fainted with shock.

There was an explosion of flashes as what sounded like hundreds of cameras all went off at once. The ridge seemed to be full of people racing toward him and Molly, all yelling and screaming and taking photo after photo. Bewildered, Neil pulled himself shakily to his feet, uncovered Molly, and looked around. Emily, Uncle Jack, and Chris were running toward him, big smiles on their faces.

"Neil!" Emily shouted, running up to him and throwing her arms around him. "Thank goodness you and Molly are safe!"

CHAPTER TEN

"Look at this one — you and Molly are on the front page!" Emily passed the newspaper to Neil, who blushed.

"I look terrible!" he complained. "I couldn't see a thing with all those flashes going off!"

Molly, who was sitting on Neil's knee, barked loudly, as if she was agreeing with him.

"You silly dog!" Neil said affectionately, rumpling her ears. "I think it's time you were trained so that you stop getting into trouble all the time!"

It was the day after Neil and Molly's great escape. Despite being cold, tired, and wet, neither of them had suffered any harm. Newspaper reporters from all over the country had been calling all morning to ask Neil questions about his ordeal, and Mrs. Wilson had come over to cook a special celebratory lunch for everyone, including Kate and Hasheem. Chris and Mrs. Wilson had also brought a stack of newspapers with them, and Neil could hardly believe how many pictures and news reports there were about him and Molly.

"This is a good one!" Chris showed Neil a large picture of himself, looking dazed, with Molly in his arms.

"I wonder if Mom and Dad will see these?" Neil said anxiously as Molly jumped off his knee to join Jake under the table. He didn't want his parents rushing back, now that the drama was over.

"I don't think they're reading the newspaper," Emily replied. "There were quite a few pictures of you and Molly when she arrived at the kennel, and Dad never mentioned seeing them when he called."

"What's the matter?" Hasheem asked. Neil continued to look anxious.

"I'm worried about what Kerry Kirby's going to say," Neil confessed. Uncle Jack had called the contact number left by Kerry as soon as Neil and Molly were safe. He hadn't been able to speak to Kerry herself, so he left a message for her. Neil hoped Kerry wasn't going to blame him for losing Molly.

"It wasn't your fault, Neil," said Kate. "I'm sure Kerry won't be angry." She stood up. "I think I'd better get back to work. Thanks for that fantastic lunch, Mrs. Wilson!"

Just then Jack came in, smiling.

"A visitor for you, Neil!" he said, and in came Mike Turner with Sam.

"Sam!"

Neil tried his best not to excite the collie too much, but he was bursting with happiness as he knelt down and put his arm around Sam's neck. Sam nuzzled against Neil's face and licked his cheek, his tail wagging furiously. He was obviously happy to be home.

"He's doing OK," Mike Turner said with a grin. "But remember what I told you. He shouldn't tire himself out."

"I know." Neil gently petted Sam's silky flanks. Molly and Jake bounced over to greet the collie. "Careful, you two! Sam's got to be treated gently!"

"And that means no underground walks!" Uncle Jack wagged a teasing finger at Neil, then rolled his eyes when the doorbell rang. "This place is like Compton Station this morning!"

"Maybe it's another reporter or photographer!" Chris grinned. "Neil's really famous now!"

"Not as famous as Molly!" Neil raised his eyebrows as Molly suddenly pricked up her ears, then shot out of the room and streaked down the hall after Uncle Jack. "What's with *her*?"

He soon found out. A moment later, Uncle Jack ushered Kerry Kirby into the room, carrying Molly in her arms. Molly was wild with joy and tugging vigorously at her mistress's dreadlocks with her teeth.

"Oh, hello, Kerry!" Neil said uncertainly. He was nervous about what the pop star might say to him, but Kerry was smiling at him reassuringly.

"I know I'm not supposed to be picking Molly up till Tuesday, but I had to come and see you both after what happened," she explained. "So I sneaked out of the hotel this morning and got Jeff to drive me down here. Rachel must be having a fit by now!"

"I'm sorry about what happened," Neil began guiltily, but Kerry shook her head at him.

"It's OK, Neil. I admit I was a little concerned when I got your uncle's message, but when I read all that stuff in the papers, I realized I should have told you not to let Molly off her leash." Kerry gave Neil a guilty grin. "She goes bananas if she spots another animal like a cat or a rabbit — she won't come back even for me!"

Neil felt better when he heard that.

"Maybe you could think about having her trained," Neil suggested politely. "Then she'd learn to come when you call her."

"Do you think so?" Kerry looked doubtful. "Molly's so high-spirited, I'm not sure it would work."

"But Molly's a smart dog," Neil said quickly. "She'd be easy to train. She learned to sit really quickly —" He stopped abruptly, hoping Kerry wouldn't mind that he'd already started training Molly.

"Can she?" Kerry looked interested and put Molly down on the floor. "Why don't you show me?"

Hoping Molly wouldn't let him down, Neil attracted the dog's attention and raised his hand. Molly immediately sat.

"That's fantastic!" Kerry said, impressed. "I didn't realize she was so fond of other dogs, too," she added as Molly and Jake began to roll around under the kitchen table together.

"Yes, it might be a good idea to get another dog to keep her company," Neil suggested eagerly.

Kerry nodded thoughtfully, then glanced at her watch. "I have to go. Rachel will be tearing her hair out by now!" She bent down and picked Molly up again.

The dog snuggled into her arms, and Kerry kissed the top of her shaggy head. "Anyway, Neil, what I really came to say was how grateful I am that you risked your life to get Molly back. Thank you so much."

"It was Molly who helped *me*, really," Neil muttered, feeling embarrassed. "I would never have found my way out again if it wasn't for her."

"But I might never have seen Molly again if it wasn't for *you*." Kerry smiled at him. "There's one more thing before I go. You have a rescue center here, don't you?"

Neil nodded.

"Well, I've been talking to the other girls in the band, and we'd like to donate something from our gig in Manchester next week to your rescue center!" Kerry announced. "To say a big thank-you!"

Everyone gasped.

"Oh, and there'll be tickets to the concert for all of you, of course!" Kerry added, and everyone gasped again.

"Wow!" Emily found her voice in front of Kerry Kirby for the first time. "And may I please have your autograph?"

"With pleasure!" Kerry handed Molly to Neil. Then she pulled a publicity photo out of her bag, signed it, and handed it to Emily.

"Bye, Molly — see you Tuesday!" She kissed Molly again and grinned at everyone else. "And I'll see you at the concert!"

"Isn't she great?" Emily said adoringly as Kerry hurried out, escorted by Uncle Jack. "I can't wait to go to the concert!"

"Looks like the Puppy Patrol's going to have even *more* money now!" Hasheem said with a grin.

"Yeah." But a shadow suddenly crossed Neil's face. It was fantastic of All Spice to donate money to the rescue center, but who would be running it in the future? It might not be the Parkers if his parents decided to leave.

"Neil?" Uncle Jack said as he came into the room again. "You're very popular this afternoon. You have some more visitors!"

He pulled the door open wider, and Bob and Carole Parker hurried in, looking dazed but smiling, and carrying a bundle of newspapers.

"Mom! Dad!" Neil gasped in disbelief as Sarah hurled herself into her mother's arms. "What're *you* doing here?"

"What do you expect when I wander down to the village shop this morning for a pint of milk and see my son plastered all over the front page?" Bob tossed the newspapers he was carrying onto the table as he swept Sarah into a bear hug. Then he looked at everyone. "Now would someone like to tell us *exactly* what's been going on?"

"A lot, by the look of it." Carole kissed Neil and then glanced anxiously at Uncle Jack's plaster cast.

Everyone started talking at once, so it took a few

minutes before Bob and Carole could piece together the whole story.

"So this is Molly." Bob squatted down and petted her. "Hello, girl!" Molly barked and stood on her hind legs, front paws on Bob's knees, wagging her tail.

"I don't know!" Carole was shaking her head in disbelief. "We go away for a few days, and everything starts happening around here!"

"You didn't have to come back early," Neil said anxiously. "We were managing OK." Although he was glad to see his parents, they'd obviously only come back because of the stories in the newspaper. He could hardly bear to ask them if they'd reached a decision about the future, but he needed to know.

"Dad," he began. "Did you — ?"

"We did." Bob smiled at him.

Neil's heart leaped. He could tell from the look on his father's face that it was good news, but he wanted to be sure before he started celebrating.

"Are we staying at King Street, Dad?" he asked in a shaky voice.

"We certainly are!" said Bob firmly.

"Yes!" Neil, Emily, Chris, and Hasheem all shouted out together as they slapped one another on the back, beaming. Mike, Mrs. Wilson, Uncle Jack, and Kate all looked thrilled, too. Only Sarah was puzzled.

"Are we going somewhere?" she asked.

"No, sweetheart. We're staying right here!" Bob said firmly.

"I'm so happy!" Kate gave Carole a hug. "This place wouldn't be the same without you!"

"We'd almost made up our minds the other way," Carole said in a shaky voice. "And then — well, we saw the newspapers this morning. How *could* we give all this up? The Parkers belong at King Street!"

Neil hugged her, too, almost too choked up with emotion to speak. "Thanks, Mom!"

Carole smiled. "And now we've got even more money to worry about spending, thanks to All Spice! Isn't it generous of them, Bob?"

Bob nodded. "Absolutely."

"What are we going to do with it all?" Neil asked eagerly. "Are we going to expand King Street?"

Bob glanced at Carole. "We've been discussing this on the drive home, although we didn't know about the All Spice money then, of course. Your mother and I have decided to go ahead and build a bigger rescue center!"

"So we can help lots more dogs!" Neil exclaimed, delighted. "Excellent!"

"We might even register it as a charity," Carole explained. "Then we can be independent of the local council because we won't need to rely on them to fund it."

"What will happen to the old rescue center?" Emily asked.

"We were thinking about turning it into a walk-in dog clinic." Bob grinned at Mike Turner. "Of course, we'd need a resident consultant there a few afternoons a week!"

"Sounds good!" Mike said eagerly. "We'll have to discuss it in detail."

"We'll be hiring another assistant, too," Carole added. "Poor Kate's overworked as it is!"

"And we've got something very special lined up for you three," laughed Bob. "We think it's only right that we go and visit Great-aunt Victoria's grave to say thank-you. So your father and I have decided that we're all going to Australia later this year!"

"Yeah!" said Emily and Sarah, and everyone began talking at once, except Neil. Instead he knelt down and picked Molly up in his arms.

"Thanks, Molly!" he said happily, hugging the little dog close. "Thanks to you, we're staying at King Street! You might be the poshest pup we've ever had staying here, but you're one of the best!"